To Tom Snowden for his excellent photographs which helped Val Biro with his illustrations.

DEDICATION

With thanks to Mary Davis for providing some useful ideas for this story and to the Round Tablers who organise the Whit Monday Fetes in the grounds of Berkhamsted Castle, which is illustrated in this book.

British Library Cataloguing in Publication Data

Todd, H.E.
The scruffy scruffy dog.
I. Title II. Biro, Val
823'.914[J] PZ7

ISBN 0-340-33192-5

First published 1983
Fourth impression 1988

Published by Hodder and Stoughton Children's Books,
a division of Hodder and Stoughton Ltd,
Mill Road, Dunton Green, Sevenoaks, Kent TN13 2YJ

Photoset by Rowland Phototypesetting Ltd,
Bury St Edmunds, Suffolk

Printed in Great Britain by Cambus Litho, East Kilbride

THE SCRUFFY SCRUFFY DOG

H. E. TODD

Illustrated by

VAL BIRO

HODDER AND STOUGHTON
LONDON SYDNEY AUCKLAND TORONTO

All the dogs in the village, except one, attended the meeting of the Lucky Puppy Club by the pond on the green.

The missing dog was a scruffy, scruffy animal whose master, Bill Baxter, was just as scruffy as he was. But no-one could ever dislike Scruffy because he always cheerfully wagged his tail.

Once he ran up wagging his tail to a fox who was about to attack some chickens. He was only trying to be friendly, but the fox ran away and all the other dogs were so relieved not to be suspected of attacking chickens that they invited him to join the Club. But he forgot to turn up.

The President of the Club was Humph (short for Humphrey). He was a famous dog because he had once frightened away a burglar, his name had been in the paper, and he had even appeared on television. He opened the meeting with an important announcement.

"On Saturday afternoon," he said, "there will be a Fete in the Castle Grounds during which there will be a Dog Show. I propose that each of us wins one event so that everyone gets a prize. All those in favour please woof."

All the members woofed.

They discussed who would win each event, and it was surprising how neatly the prizes could be shared.
But then Fifi, the pretty poodle who barked with a French accent and smelt of lavender, asked a difficult question:
"What about Scruffy? I know he has forgotten to come to this meeting, but he is so good-natured and he has never won a prize in his life. I am sure that, if he could, he would be much more sensible afterwards."
Fifi knew how to behave properly. She belonged to Lady Fitzherbert, an important local personage.
All the dogs agreed.

The trouble was – what could Scruffy possibly win? He wasn't very long or short. He wasn't very pretty. He wasn't very clean. In fact he wasn't anything in particular, except Scruffy! In any case the only prize left was for The Most Obedient Dog, and Scruffy certainly wasn't very obedient!

"There's only one solution," said Humph. "For that event we shall all have to be more disobedient than Scruffy. And any dog who cheats by behaving well will be expelled from the Club."

So that was that.

Saturday afternoon was fine, and there was a big crowd at the Dog Show. The judge was Colonel Danvers, an impressive-looking gentleman with a red face and a bristly moustache.

Everything went exactly as planned by the dogs.

Scamp, the wire-haired terrier, cocked his head on one side, with such a perky expression on his face, that he easily won the Cheekiest Dog Prize. It was ideal for him – a wire hairbrush!

Shaggy was the Shaggiest Dog and was presented with some shampoo powder.

Dibs and Dabs, the twin puppies, were obviously the Tiniest Dogs. They won a bouncing ball between them, and when they played with it afterwards it was difficult to decide which bounced higher, the ball or the puppies.

By far the fattest was Sally, a greedy black spaniel, and she was given a bag of biscuits to make her fatter still.

Sausage and Mash, very, very long brothers, each wanted to be the l o n g e s t dog. Sausage cheated by sticking his tongue out at the front, but Mash got his own back, by sticking his tail out at the rear. It was decided that they were of equal length and they won half a sausage each.

As expected, Fifi was the Prettiest Dog. After receiving a bottle of lavender water she paraded charmingly with Lady Fitzherbert.

Humph surpassed himself. He sat up tall and straight with the Best Beg. Colonel Danvers put his prize of a bar of chocolate on his nose *and* he tossed it in the air and caught it in his mouth.

By now it was almost time for the important event of the afternoon, the Most Obedient Dog. But where was Scruffy? He had completely disappeared! All the dogs were *very* worried.

Then cries and loud barking could be heard coming from the Castle moat. Sitting on the bank was a little girl sobbing bitterly because her beautiful coloured beach ball had bounced into the water. Scruffy had bounded in to rescue it and was having great fun pushing it in all directions with his nose.

"Come here at once, Scruffy," yelled Bill Baxter. It was just as well that the Most Obedient Dog competition had not started because Scruffy took not the slightest notice and went on playing his game. In the end Bill Baxter had to wade into the moat and haul out Scruffy and the ball.

The little girl was delighted to get her ball back, but Bill Baxter was furious because they were in such a filthy state for the competition which was just about to start.

And that was when the members of the Lucky Puppy Club showed just how clever they could be.

Scamp did nothing but twirl round and round chasing his own tail

till everyone became quite giddy looking at him.

Shaggy pretended not to be able to see through the hair in front of her eyes, and blundered about barging into people.

Dibs and Dabs started a mock fight and snarled so furiously at each other that they had to be separated.

Sally fell fast asleep and never went into the ring at all!

Sausage and Mash dug for rats that weren't there, and the louder they were ordered to stop digging, the deeper they dug till

only their tails could be seen.

By then everyone in the crowd was laughing and it was time for Scruffy and his master to appear. And what an appearance they made! The crowd laughed even louder and the dogs were anxious for Scruffy not to be silly again.

There was no need to worry because for once Bill Baxter had a brainwave. He ordered Scruffy to wag his tail.

Scruffy did not understand a word, but he always wagged his tail anyway, so there he was being obedient by accident!

There were still two dogs to come, and their owners were confident of success. How wrong they were!

"Come along, Fifi darling," said Lady Fitzherbert, "hold up your paw and shake hands with the nice man."

Fifi turned her back and started to scratch herself. "Don't be silly, Fifi darling," said Lady Fitzherbert, "nice dogs don't scratch."

But Fifi just scratched herself harder, and went on scratching until her red-faced mistress carried her from the ring amidst roars of laughter.

Now for the President. Surely he would behave himself?
Not a bit of it. Humph trotted right across the ring and bit
the judge on the leg. It was purposely only a
soft bite that could not possibly harm anyone,

but Colonel Danvers hopped about
making such a furious fuss that Humph
felt dearly like biting his other leg for him!

So Scruffy was the winner of the Most Obedient Dog competition after all, even if he *was* covered with mud and *had* only been obedient by accident! And Humph's clever plan for every dog to win a prize had worked perfectly.

Colonel Danvers presented Scruffy with his prize which was a smart red leather collar, amidst great applause from the crowd.